The Graves Family

THOSE WHO MARCH TO A DIFFERENT DRUMMER
ARE IN A MAGNIFICENT BAND INDEED!

Patricia Polacco
The Graves Family

Philomel Books

No one saw them slide into Union City that dark and dreary night. Doug and Shalleaux Graves arrived with their family of five children to take up residence in the old house on Park Street. The town clock struck wildly and ran backwards, and the water in the fountain in the village square turned crimson as their car drove by.

The first thing the new family did was to paint the house bloodred! No one in the village even considered visiting them after that. Even the post-man left their mail at the curb.

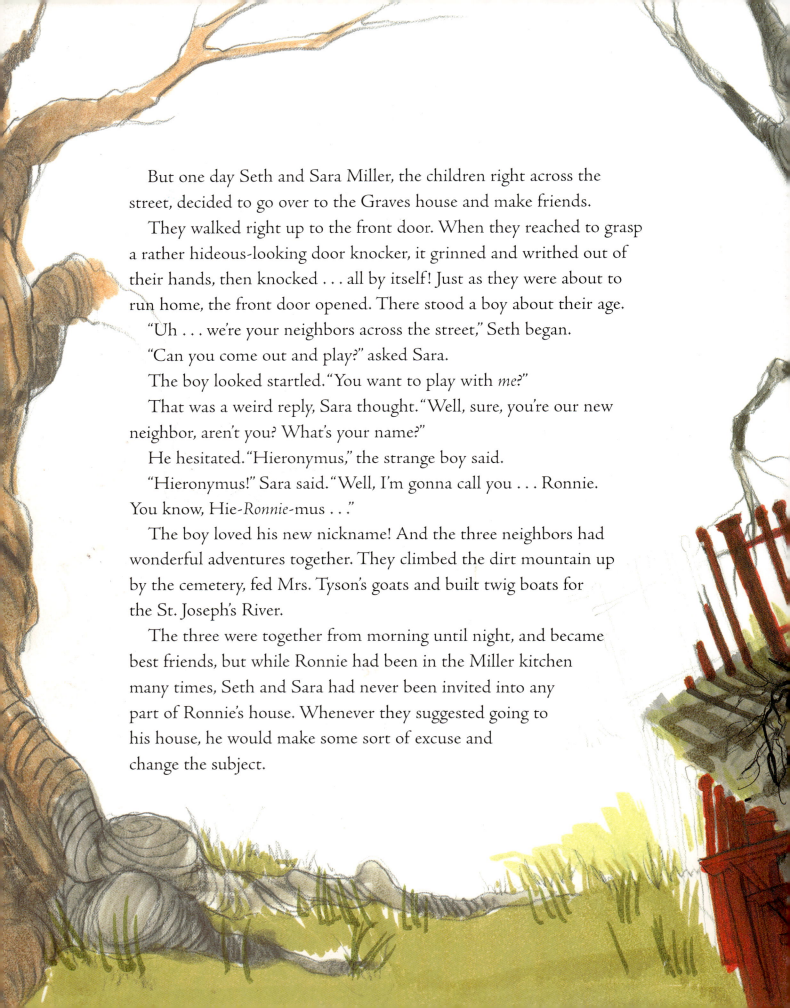

But one day Seth and Sara Miller, the children right across the street, decided to go over to the Graves house and make friends.

They walked right up to the front door. When they reached to grasp a rather hideous-looking door knocker, it grinned and writhed out of their hands, then knocked . . . all by itself! Just as they were about to run home, the front door opened. There stood a boy about their age.

"Uh . . . we're your neighbors across the street," Seth began.

"Can you come out and play?" asked Sara.

The boy looked startled. "You want to play with *me?*"

That was a weird reply, Sara thought. "Well, sure, you're our new neighbor, aren't you? What's your name?"

He hesitated. "Hieronymus," the strange boy said.

"Hieronymus!" Sara said. "Well, I'm gonna call you . . . Ronnie. You know, Hie-*Ronnie*-mus . . ."

The boy loved his new nickname! And the three neighbors had wonderful adventures together. They climbed the dirt mountain up by the cemetery, fed Mrs. Tyson's goats and built twig boats for the St. Joseph's River.

The three were together from morning until night, and became best friends, but while Ronnie had been in the Miller kitchen many times, Seth and Sara had never been invited into any part of Ronnie's house. Whenever they suggested going to his house, he would make some sort of excuse and change the subject.

FINALLY, THOUGH, the day came when Ronnie asked Sara and Seth over to play. His parents weren't home, and he was baby-sitting his four little sisters. He could use the company, he said.

"The Graves seem to be nice enough people, a little strange perhaps, but nice enough," Mrs. Miller said when Seth and Sara asked if it was okay.

So on that day Seth and Sara went.

"Come in," a voice said when they knocked. But when they entered, a dark cloud of flying things whirled around their heads, then darted upstairs. Huge plants and musty flowers were everywhere—but all dead. Two robed skeletons leered at them near two chairs piled with huge, fluffy pillows. And the walls seemed to be painted a strange, dull black.

As their eyes adjusted to the dark, they realized the walls were alive with . . .

"Spiders," Sara gasped, when suddenly Ronnie appeared in front of them.

"They are perfectly harmless," he assured them. "My father is not only an inventor and scientist, but an amateur entomologist. He collects endangered bugs and spiders from all over the world. He feels that by giving them the run of the house, they are happier.

"I was just fixing lunch for my sisters. Come and meet them."

Sara and Seth walked more slowly now. The kitchen was filled with pots and pans, hanging from the ceiling, surrounding the stove.

"My mother is a gourmet cook," Ronnie said, sitting down at the table beside four little redheaded girls—all the same age. "And these are Billicent, Cintilla, Congolia and Tondileo." They were all eating peanut butter sandwiches.

But behind them was a strange-looking plant, with leaves like tentacles.

"I've never seen anything like this," Sara said as she moved closer, when suddenly the plant lunged at her!

"Her name is Phoebe. A rare and unknown Venus flytrap. Just a baby. She thinks you're going to feed her," Ronnie said as he popped a piece of sandwich into one of Phoebe's gaping mouths. "My mother raised her from a single cutting my father brought back from the wilds of Peru."

Sara watched as Phoebe snatched a giant fly in midflight. She gulped.

"My mother isn't exactly great with regular plants and flowers, but she has a veritable green thumb when it comes to Venus flytraps," Ronnie said. "My father is the genius, though. Would you like to see his laboratory?"

They followed Ronnie into the basement. Everywhere they looked were bubbling beakers, hissing gauges, flashing lights and buzzing buttons with curling glass tubes running from one to another.

Ronnie placed a small beaker of green liquid in front of them, then placed a peach next to it. "Here's his biggest experiment ever—it's top secret. If I show you, you can't tell anyone about it. Swear on a dead toad?"

"Yes," Sara and Seth agreed.

Ronnie took a small dropper and dripped three drops of the liquid onto the peach. It just sat there for a while. But then the peach seemed to puff up, and before their eyes, gobs of peach fuzz started growing longer and longer and longer until it became bushy, thick hair.

"Man, oh, man, if this stuff can grow hair on a peach, think what it could do for all of the old bald geezers in this town," Seth crowed. "How did he discover this stuff?"

"House cats. He noticed that no matter how much they shed, their fur grows back twofold . . . only to shed again."

"So he figured out the secret of how house cats grow back their fur?" Sara asked.

"Yes. He extracted an enzyme from the follicles of their hair . . . he won't even tell us what!"

"Oh, dear," said Sara. "Does it hurt the cats?"

Ronnie laughed. "Not a bit." He held up a bottle and gazed at it. "My father is still perfecting it, though. What he knows right now for sure is that this formula causes hair to grow on anything."

Just then two voices called from upstairs: "Children, we're home."

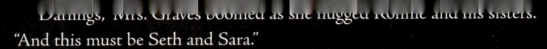

Darlings," Mrs. Graves boomed as she hugged Ronnie and his sisters. "And this must be Seth and Sara."

"Greetings, greetings," said Dr. Graves cheerfully as he went right to the basement door. "I must away to the laboratory."

"Your father and I shopped all day to find exactly the right type of blistered variegated turnip. I am just dying to try a new recipe that I thought up today," she said as she floated into the kitchen.

But just then all of the fluffy pillows jumped off the chairs and trotted into the kitchen after her. Seth and Sara gasped. The fluffy pillows were the hairiest, most repulsive, biggest spiders they had ever seen.

"Come along, my dearest pookie wookie doodles," Mrs. Graves cooed as the spiders jumped around her, doing tricks. "And perhaps you children would like to come for dinner tonight."

Sara and Seth gulped.

"Please come," Ronnie said excitedly.

"We'll . . . we'll ask," Sara said.

"Be back at six," Mrs. Graves said as she clanged the pots and pans and put on a chef's cap.

When Sara and Seth told their mother about the Graves' house, and about spiders on the walls and the Venus flytrap, she just winked at them as if they were pulling her leg. And when they told her about how Mrs. Graves was a gardener and a cook and a little odd, she only heard "gardener and cook."

So when they said Mrs. Graves had asked them to supper, Mrs. Miller said, "How nice. Of course you can go to dinner, and I am going to invite her to the Garden Club Tea," and she cut some flowers from her garden for Seth to take to Mrs. Graves.

Just as the children walked in the front door, a loud explosion rocked the house. Plaster fell off the ceiling and spiders ran in panic. A puff of acrid-smelling fumes wafted up out of the floor registers.

"Lovie, I think I have gotten the formula very nearly right this time!" Dr. Graves sang out as he bounded up the basement stairs.

"Just in time for dinner, dear!" Mrs. Graves announced as she gestured for everyone to join her in the dining room.

"These are for you," Seth said as he handed her the bouquet his mother had sent. But as she took them, every flower turned brown, dried out and instantly withered.

"Thank you," Mrs. Graves said as she put the flowers in a vase and placed them on the table as if nothing at all had happened to them.

Everyone gathered around the table. Dr. Graves rubbed his hands together enthusiastically.

"Tonight's menu is . . ." Mrs. Graves uncovered each serving dish. "Great New Zealand Land Vipers with Capers and Clotted Cream, Pureed Lampfish Fins with Bees' Knees and Guppy Fillets, Parasitic Lamprey Spines with Spotted Eel in Tamarillo Aspic from Madagascar, Boiled Blistered Variegated Turnip Root from right here . . . and Indonesian Snarling Knishes Au Gratin, garnished with Octopus Knuckles from Tibet!"

That is when Seth and Sara noticed Phoebe. She had grown even bigger since that afternoon.

"And Beetle Leg Jell-O with Fly Carcass for Phoebe!" Mrs. Graves said as the giant flytrap flailed its arms and devoured its dinner, plates and all.

Everyone set to eating their supper with relish and glee, all but Seth and Sara. They just sat and stared at their plates. Their food was moving!

"Oh, dear me," Mrs. Graves said as her eyes filled with tears. "You don't like it. Poor Hieronymus, just when you finally made some friends, I've spoiled everything."

"Oh, Mrs. Graves, please don't cry," Sara begged. "It's just that this food is a little unusual for us. That's all." The food was still moving.

"We've moved from town to town, always at night, always hoping to make a fresh start," Dr. Graves said sadly. "But something always seems to happen."

"You're different," Seth said, "but we like that you're different. My mother even sent along this invitation for the Garden Club Tea."

Mrs. Graves eagerly opened it; her eyes widened and she shrieked with joy. "'The Union City Ladies Auxiliary Garden Club cordially invites you to attend a Tea on Saturday at the home of Mrs. Apassionata Trenchmouth!'" she sang out as she danced around the room. "'Bring a plant to share.' Oh, my dears, maybe at long last we'll fit in."

After all, Sara thought, what could happen at the Union City Ladies Garden Club Tea?

ON SATURDAY, Mrs. Miller and Mrs. Graves arrived for the Tea on time. Mrs. Graves had put on her best outfit for the occasion and brought along one of Phoebe's babies in a covered carrier.

Her heart was full of happiness.

She and Mrs. Miller had had two cups of tea and had heard about Mrs. Saspilla's black-eyed Susans, Miss Delilah's giant delphiniums and Mary Pigeonpie's double petunias when Doretta Dovetonsil trotted through the front door, out of breath. "Guess who is coming to judge the Fall Home Show this year!"

"Who?" the collected women gasped.

"Christopher Joel," she trumpeted, and collapsed in a swoon.

Christopher Joel had the most popular television show on home decorating of all time—broadcast all the way from Hollywood. "He is bringing a photographer from the *Ladies Lovely Home Companion*," Doretta Dovetonsil went on. "And there will be a cash prize for the Best Decorated House of the Year."

With a lift of an eyebrow, a subtle shift of a gaze, every lady in the room was filling herself full of murderous resolve to be the one whose house would be picked by Christopher Joel, when there was a piercing scream.

Mrs. Pissasperoy's hybrid rose tree, a grand champion at the state flower show, had wilted. Mrs. Dovetonsil's tea roses were dead as doornails. Mrs. Trenchmouth was holding her limp and withered orchids.

Mrs. Graves had slipped away, and was moving through the garden. As she did, each plant and shrub she paused by dried, withered and died.

"It's her!" the ladies screamed, but as they surrounded Mrs. Graves, the small Venus flytrap had an untimely growth spurt and burst out of its carrier. It grabbed voraciously at lemon squares, the tea set, the Persian rugs . . . it devoured everything that was not sitting down. And then it lurched at the Union City Garden Club members' hats and ate every one.

Mrs. Graves made a hasty retreat. "One more disaster," she muttered. "We'll never fit in."

From that moment on, the happening was referred to by the ladies in the Union City Garden Club as the Great Flytrap Affair.

DESPITE THE UNPLEASANTNESS and scandal at the Union City Garden Club Tea, Union City was in full swing, making preparations for the Fall Home Show and for the arrival of Christopher Joel. Everyone was vying for the coveted honor of having the Best Decorated House of the Year. All but Mrs. Graves.

She had taken to her bed with the shame of it all. Seth, Sara and Ronnie tried to cheer her up, but she was inconsolable.

"Poor Mother," Ronnie said to his father. "What can we do to help?"

"Hmmm," said his father. "Perhaps if we could do something for the town, people would forget the Garden Tea incident. Something so . . . so . . . significant, we would be accepted here in Union City."

"Yes! We've got to come up with something," Ronnie said thoughtfully.

All of them thought and thought. Finally Seth sprang out of his chair. "I know! Haven't you all noticed how many old geezers in this town are bald?" Everyone nodded yes. "Well, wouldn't they do just about anything to have their hair again?"

"Of course," Sara exploded. "Dr. Graves . . . your secret formula."

"Father, they're right. Think of what you could do for all of those Union City men!" Ronnie said.

Dr. Graves rose and paced the floor. "The formula hasn't been fully tested quite yet . . . but it has successfully grown hair on just about anything."

"Dr. Graves, you have to do it for Mrs. Graves," Seth said urgently.

"By Jove . . . I do believe you're right. For Mrs. Graves! Let's away to the laboratory!" he shouted as he made for the basement door.

The children helped Dr. Graves mix up a fresh batch of his magic hair-growing formula. They filled thirty-seven small but important bottles and took them to town three days before the Annual Fall Home Show. Then they gave them out on the corner of Main and Coldwater to Mayor Trenchmouth, Mr. Pissasperoy, Mr. Dovetonsil, most of the town council— anyone whose pate was poking through.

Well, sir, Dr. Graves' formula was a complete success. The results were

better than hoped for. Every bald man in town was asking for a bottle of Dr. Graves' Famous Hair-Raising Elixir. The villagers forgot the Great Flytrap Affair. Even Mrs. Graves was held in good stead once again.

And it put everyone in the best mood for the Fall Home Show. As the show grew closer, the air was positively electric with dreams of winning the coveted Best Decorated House Award and being featured in the *Ladies Lovely Home Companion*.

FINALLY THE BIG DAY arrived, and so did Christopher Joel, all the way from Hollywood. Every home in town had manicured lawns, flower displays on their porches next to old rockers and antique wheelbarrows and such.

Mayor Trenchmouth and the town council accompanied Mr. Joel to each and every house. But Mr. Joel made comments that never exceeded "Ah, very nice . . . very nice," and then he'd yawn.

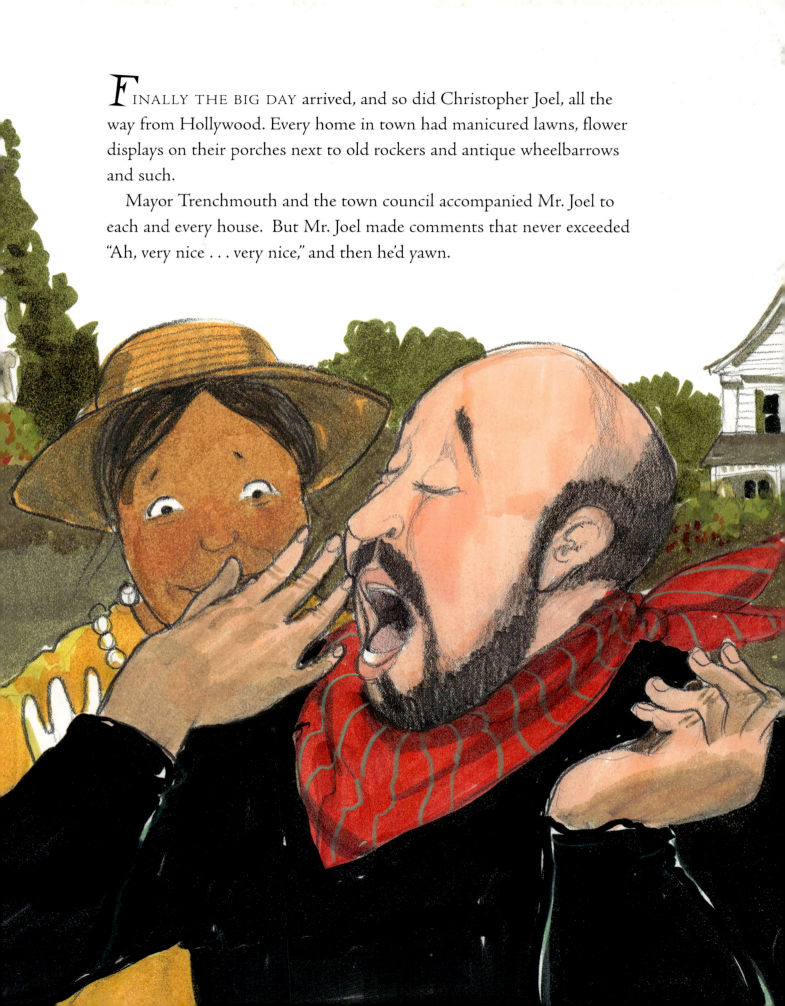

It was at Mrs. Dovetonsil's house that Mayor Trenchmouth got a strange look on his face. He twitched, his eyes widened, then he dropped to all fours and sharpened his nails on a doormat. Suddenly a leaf blown by the wind caught his eye, and he raced after it, pouncing on it over and over again.

Then he stopped and scratched his ear with his left leg.

At exactly that moment, all of the men on the town council and men's club, formerly bald to a man but now full-toffed, fell to their hands and knees as well. One of them hissed at another. Mr. Pissasperoy stalked a bird in a tree next to the street. Then he froze and made a chattering sound with his mouth as he watched the bird.

Mr. Pitkimple darted under a porch carpet and batted at the ankles of his wife, who stood helplessly watching. Then Mr. Dovetonsil himself seized a scarecrow off a porch rocker and, lying on his back, rabbit-kicked it while he held it between his teeth and arms.

Three men on the town council, a usually silent three, had treed them-
selves and were meowing and howling in chorus. The fire brigade had to be
called to get them out of the tree. Even the bank president, Mr. Greenbill,
crouched next to a mouse hole and refused to leave it.

"Ronnie!" Seth whispered. "There must be something in that hair stuff
that makes them act this way."

"Yes!" they all shouted, and the three of them scampered for home.

They arrived at the Graves' house completely out of breath. "We have a disaster!" they said breathlessly.

"I should say we have," Dr. Graves said as he and Mrs. Graves tried to stop a flow of viscous blue goo that was oozing from the kitchen. "I guess my new soap formula was a little too . . . enthusiastic . . . for the dishwasher," Dr. Graves said sheepishly.

"No, Father, we're talking about the mayor and the men on the council," Ronnie cried. "All the bald men who used your formula are crawling around, acting like house cats!"

"An angry mob is heading this way!" Seth announced.

"We're ruined!" Mrs. Graves wailed as she held her head.

At that exact moment, the front door opened and a wall of screaming angry wives flowed in. They were met with a whirling cloud of bats. As the ladies rushed the house, they landed in the living room and slipped on the nasty blue formula, which held them fast. They could hardly move. The giant spiders inched all over them as they screamed in terror.

Then something in a very large pot in the kitchen pushed off the lid and

crawled toward them. It was Phoebe, who then pulled herself into the room and managed to kiss each person in the room with all of her mouths.

Mrs. Trenchmouth fainted. Mrs. Pissasperoy had an attack of the vapors.

"She is such an affectionate flytrap," Mrs. Graves cooed.

"What kind of a madhouse is this?!" the angry mob screamed, at which Mrs. Graves began to sob uncontrollably.

"I'll tell you what kind of a madhouse this is," Christopher Joel roared as he pushed his way through the crowd outside. "It's the most perfect haunted house that I have ever seen. I love this. I love this!" he cried as he went from room to room.

Everyone was speechless.

"You mean you like this?" Mrs. Graves asked in total disbelief.

"Like it? I adore it!" Mr. Joel said as he slid around the rooms on the blue, gloppy mess. "I have never seen such terrifying décor . . . ever!"

Sara, Seth and the Graves family beamed. The townsfolk gave each other looks.

"Take lots of pictures. This is not only going to be our lead article, but our cover story!" the publisher of the *Ladies Lovely Home Companion* called out.

"I'm going to have you all on my show!" Mr. Joel sang out as he petted a giant spider.

Needless to say, the Graves house won the Fall Home Show. As for the mayor and the town council, they were hospitalized and treated for fleas. The effects of the hair formula eventually wore off, as did their full heads of hair.

And the village? It has grown to be quite proud of the Graves family and their wonderful "haunted house." When people ask about the Graves and their house on the hill, villagers say, "Well, they fit in. They just fit in."

PATRICIA LEE GAUCH, EDITOR

Text and illustrations copyright © 2003 by Babushka, Inc.

Manufactured in China by South China Printing Co. Ltd.
Designed by Semadar Megged. Text set in 15-point Adobe Jenson. The art was done in pencil and watercolor.
Library of Congress Cataloging-in-Publication Data
Polacco, Patricia. The Graves family / Patricia Polacco ; Patricia Lee Gauch, ed. p. cm. Summary: When the spooky Graves family moves to town and tries to fit in with the "normal" residents of Union City, everyone is in for a few surprises. [1. Moving, Household—Fiction. 2. Haunted houses—Fiction.] I. Gauch, Patricia Lee. II. Title. PZ7.P75186 Gr 2003 [Fic]—dc21 2002154487

ISBN 0-399-24034-9
5 7 9 10 8 6